My Dad
Takes Care
Of Me

Story by Patricia Quinlan • Art by Vlasta van Kampen

Annick Press
Toronto • New York

Fifth printing, November 1995

Annick Press Ltd.

Annick Press gratefully acknowledges the support of the Canada Council and the Ontario Arts Council.

Canadian Cataloguing in Publication Data
Quinlan, Patricia
  My dad takes care of me

  ISBN 0-920303-79-X (bound) ISBN 0-920303-76-5 (pbk.)

  I. Van Kampen, Vlasta. II. Title.

  PS8583.U55Mps 1987 jC813'.54 C86-095071-9
  PZ7.Q55My 1987

CURR
PZ
7
Q55
My
1987

The art in this book was rendered in watercolours.
The text was typeset in Bookman.

Distributed in Canada by:
Firefly Books Ltd.
250 Sparks Avenue
Willowdale, ON
M2H 2S4

Published in the U.S.A. by Annick Press (U.S.) Ltd.
Distributed in the U.S.A. by:
Firefly Books (U.S.) Inc.
P.O. Box 1338
Ellicott Station
Buffalo, NY 14205

∞ Printed on acid-free paper.

Printed and bound in Canada by Friesens, Altona, Manitoba.

For Paul and Jillian

My stomach hurt when the kids in school asked, "What does your dad do?"

I didn't know what to say, so I said, "He's a pilot."

Sometimes I'm glad my dad doesn't have a job. When I come home at lunch he makes me soup.

I can go straight home after school instead of to the babysitter's. My dad plays games with me before supper. I help him cook.

My dad and I talk about more things now. Like the way I feel when I ride my bike fast. I told him, "A big kid at school punched me. I was afraid to hit him back."

"Sometimes I'm afraid of things too, Luke," he said.

My dad used to work in a factory where they made cars. The factory closed and my dad lost his job. My friend Paul's dad lost his job too. I asked my dad why the factory closed. He said it closed because people didn't buy enough cars from his company.

We used to live in a town in the country. We had a house with a big back yard. There was a stream where my dad and I went fishing. After my dad's factory closed, my mom got a new job and we moved to the city. Now we live in an apartment. Across the street there's a park. It has a pool where I go swimming with my friends.

I had fun living in the country but I like living in the city too.

My mom works with computers. Often she has to work at night. I'm glad my dad is home to read me stories and tuck me in. I told him, "I have bad dreams about monsters who chase me."

"There are times when I have bad dreams too," he said.

My dad gets angry sometimes. When I asked him for a new bike, he said, "We can't afford it, Luke."

"I wish you had a job," I said.

"I want a job," he said. "But there aren't enough jobs for everyone who wants one."

My dad gets sad, too. One day I came home after school and he was crying. My mom said it was because he didn't get the job he wanted. I told him, "It's okay, I love you, Daddy!" My dad hugged me real hard. "I love you very much, Luke," he said.

My dad wants to be an accountant. He goes to school now too, only by mail. He mails his homework to his teacher and his teacher marks it and sends it back. Sometimes we do our homework together. My dad said, "I think math is hard, Luke."

I told him,
"I know what you mean, Dad."

Jillian's a new girl in my class. I went to her house after school. Her dad was home. I asked him, "Do you have a job?"

"Yes, I have a job," he said. "My job is taking care of Jillian."

I don't like my dad to be sad, so I hope he gets a job he wants. But I like my dad being at home.
My stomach doesn't hurt any more when the kids in school ask, "What does your dad do?"

I tell them,
"My dad takes care of me."